Nick's Birthday Surprise

ISBN 0-7696-4188-1

5 0 3 9 5

9 780769 641881

EAN

School Specialty
Publishing

Text Copyright © Evans Brothers Ltd. 2005. Illustration Copyright ©
Evans Brothers Ltd. 2005. First published by Evans Brothers Limited, 2A
Portman Mansions, Chiltern Street, London W1U 6NR, United
Kingdom. This edition published under license from Zero to Ten
Limited. All rights reserved. Printed in China. This edition published in
2005 by Gingham Dog Press, an imprint of School Specialty Publishing,
a member of the School Specialty Family.

Library of Congress-in-Publication Data is on file with the publisher.

Sent all inquiries to:
School Specialty Publishing
8720 Orion Place
Columbus, OH 43240-2111

ISBN 0-7696-4188-1

1 2 3 4 5 6 7 8 9 10 EVN 10 09 08 07 06 05

Nick's Birthday Surprise

By Jane Oliver

Illustrated by Silvia Raga

GINGHAM DOG
PRESS

Columbus, Ohio

Happy Birthday, Nick!

3

6

Nick gets big presents and small presents.

What is this?

Seeds!

Nick plants them.

12

13

He waters them.

He waits.

17

18

He watches.

19

Nick forgets about them.

Surprise!

The seeds start
to grow.

They grow into plants.

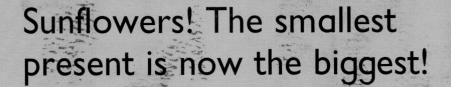

Sunflowers! The smallest
present is now the biggest!

Nick wins a prize!

Words I Know

birthday	small
presents	plants
waters	watches
seeds	surprise

Think About It!

1. What was in the smallest present?
2. How do you know that Nick took care of his plants?
3. Why do you think that he forgot about them?
4. What was the surprise?

The Story and You

1. Have you ever had a surprise birthday present? What was it?
2. Did you ever plant something and watch it grow? Tell about it.
3. What is your favorite flower? Why?